A DROP OF THE SEA

For all the dreamers, big and small — I.C.

A DROP OF THE SEA

Ingrid Chabbert ▪ Guridi

Kids Can Press

Ali lives at the edge of the desert, not far from a hundred-year-old palm tree. He likes climbing it to snack on fresh dates. He never forgets to pick a few for his great-grandmother, too.

At night, on the roof of their tiny clay house, they wonder at the infinity of the starry sky. Just her and him. Just him and her.

They don't need anything more to be happy.
But Ali has grown worried the last few weeks.
In her old age, his great-grandmother is finding
it harder to walk. He has noticed she is breathless
and wincing at every step.

Settled on her stool, her gaze lost on the horizon,
she looks like she's a thousand years old.
And Ali knows people can't grow that old.
Only the desert and palm trees can.

At her side, he asks softly, "Great-grandma, have all of your dreams come true?"
Surprised, she looks at him, and sighs.

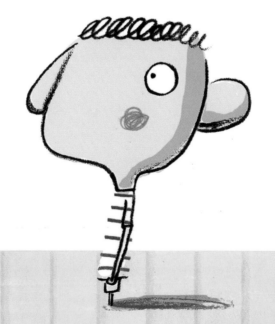

"You don't want to answer?"

"I do, my dear Ali. I was thinking …"

"So tell me, then. The truth."

"I think all of my little-girl and grown-up dreams have come true. Except …"

"Except?"

"Except my dream to see the sea. I could have — it isn't so far, two days' walk at the most. But I always put it off to another time and, now, my poor legs can't carry me there."

Ali sighs in turn and sits quietly as the night gathers around them.

The next day at first light, a determined Ali declares:
"Great-grandmother, I am going to seek the sea for you."
A breathless laugh escapes the old woman's lips.
"Come now, Ali, you are too young. It's a long way."
"My mind is made up — I'm going. If all goes well, I'll be back in four days."

With a pail in hand and a pack full of dates and water, Ali sets off without looking back. He wouldn't want to see his great-grandmother's tears wet the dry dirt. Or for her to see his, maybe.

She is right. Ali will need a bit less than two days to reach his destination.

He walks as quickly as his little legs will go.

He spends a near-frightening night under an unfamiliar palm tree.

Then Ali sees it.

There, in front of him — the sea.

Serenely calm, it licks at his aching toes.

In that moment, he would love to be holding his great-grandmother's hand and watching her eyes dive into the blue of the sea.

He sits awhile, contemplating it.

But not for too long — one doesn't keep great-grandmothers waiting.

He begins to fill his pail, as carefully as if he were handling crystal.

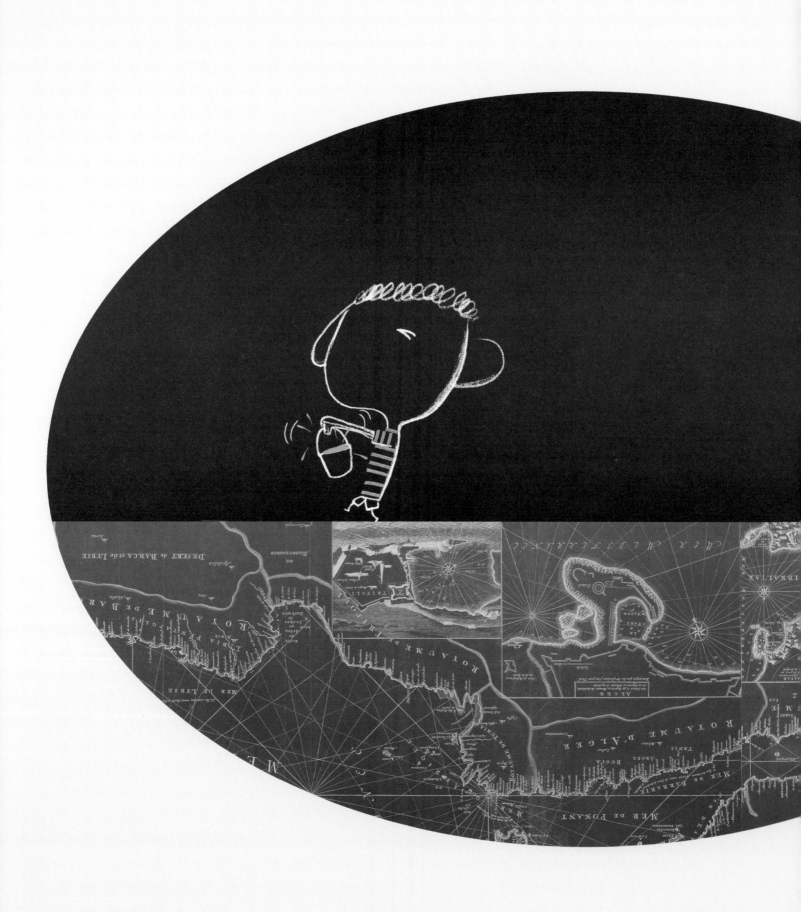

And it's with pail in hand, heavy at the end of his arm, pack in tow, that Ali sets off again without looking back.

He doesn't want to see the sea stealing after him on the sand.

The walk home will take him a bit more than two days.
He imagines his great-grandmother on her stool,
squinting to see the tiny dot he must be on the horizon.
And at last, he is running into her arms.
He has missed her scent.
Gently pulling away, he offers her the pail.

At the very bottom, only a few drops of the sea remain.
The long walk and heat got the better of the treasure.
The old woman rolls one of the drops between her
fingers and starts to cry. "Oh, Ali, this is one of the most
beautiful days of my life!"

The boy's heart soars.

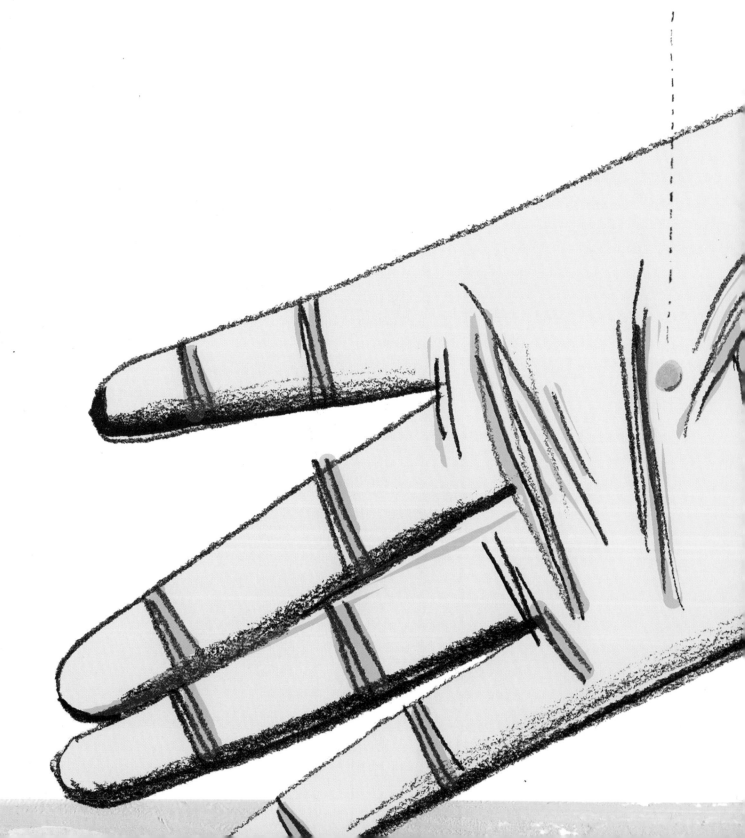

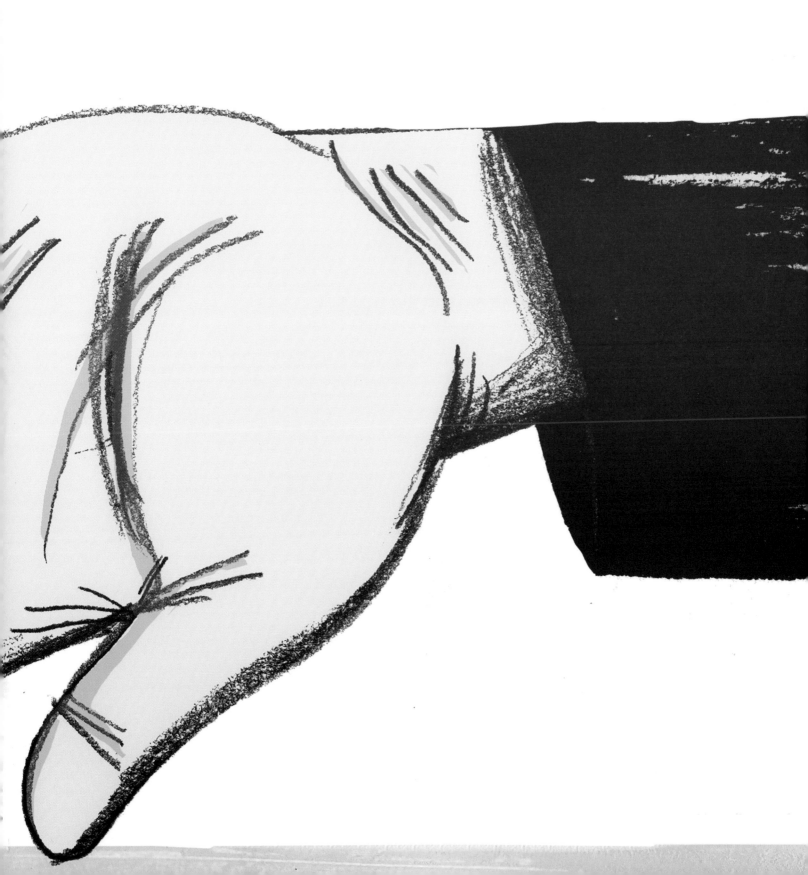

That night on the roof of their tiny clay house,
Ali tells his great-grandmother about the sea,
again and again.

This edition published by Kids Can Press in 2018

Originally published in France under the title *Un bout de mer*
by Éditions Frimousse.

Kids Can Press gratefully acknowledges the financial support of the
Government of Ontario, through the Ontario Media Development Corporation.

Published in Canada and the U.S. by Kids Can Press Ltd.
25 Dockside Drive, Toronto, ON M5A 0B5

Kids Can Press is a Corus Entertainment Inc. company

www.kidscanpress.com

The artwork in this book was rendered digitally and in gouache and pencil.
The text is set in ITC Lubalin Graph.

English edition edited by Yvette Ghione

Printed and bound in Shenzhen, China, in 3/2018 by C & C Offset

CM 18 0 9 8 7 6 5 4 3 2 1

Library and Archives Canada Cataloguing in Publication

Chabbert, Ingrid, 1978–
[Bout de mer. English]
        A drop of the sea / Ingrid Chabbert, Guridi.

Translation of: Un bout de mer.
ISBN 978-1-5253-0124-7 (hardcover)

        I. Nieto Guridi, Raúl, 1970–, illustrator II. Title.
III. Title: Bout de mer. English.

PZ7.C349Dro 2018   j843'.92   C2018-900629-3